THREE TALES

Christopher Laverty

CONTENTS

THE MISFORTUNE OF REYNOLD THE KNIGHT

From a story by Boccaccio

O fortune – how she is a fickle child;
our trusty chronicles show all too well
how she would bless the souls on whom she smiled -
then throw them to the wild with wolves to dwell.
Yet sometimes all ends well, and I can tell
if you've an ear – a tale – set in our land -
of fortune springing from misfortune's hand.

It was the age of knights and ladies, passion
and fealty – honourable death and shame -
monastic reveries and courtly fashion.
One knight there was – throughout the land his fame
was greatly spoke of – Reynold was his name.
One evening he homewards rode – past inns -
past countryside – and here our tale begins.

Now cold it was, all day it had been snowing;
the sky was crisp, the stars were sharp, the moon
hung low and clear. Steadily he was going
as gallant Reynold rode all afternoon.

One serving-man accompanied him – but soon
he fell in with a passing company,
conversing with the folk unwarily.

He thought them merchants – well attired and
coined,
and warmly ordering themselves to him,
but these in truth were robbers he had joined.
They spoke like humble men of toil and hymn,
and sought to gain his trust as it grew dim;
they, judging him a moneyed fellow, waited -
until they spied a woodlands isolated.

They fell to talk of orisons they make -
one of the highwaymen then asked our friend:
'Which say you on your journeys, when you wake?'
'I am a simple man', said he, 'and tend
to live old-fashioned; nevertheless, I'll send
St Julian a Pater and an Ave -
to grant in perils somewhere safe to stay'.

'I hope it stands you in good stead', then thought
the highwayman that asked. 'This orison',
said he, 'I've heard of but was never taught -
and always found I lodgings after Sun.
No, De Profundiis is for me the one,
the prayer that my grandmother deemed the best -
and later we shall see who'll find good rest.'

Discoursing of these matters on their way,
while waiting for a quiet place and time,
they came across a river – late that day,
beyond which distant spires stood sublime,
and here the robbers carried out their crime.
Stealing his money, clothes and horse, they departed,
saying – while turning back with laughs
wholehearted -

'We hope St Julian for you will find
good lodgings for tonight, even as ours.'.
Passing the river, they left him behind,
stood only in his shirt at those late hours,
far from the church's gleaming gothic towers -
while Reynold's knavish servant, turning his horse -
abandoned him – and townwards steered his course.

Poor Reynold - trembling with his teeth - he turned
and looked about for shelter from the frost;
but war had been there in those parts, and burned
was everything. Instead, the stream he crossed,
and sought the town, while fearing getting lost.
But curfew fell and he arrived so late,
he found they'd raised the bridge and shut the gate.

There, shivering and disconsolate he stood -
as it began once more that day to snow;

he spied an outhouse building made of wood
projecting from the wall. The warming glow
of fires within he saw from down below.
Once there, the door was locked - although he found
a bed of straw, and lay there on the ground.

He sighed – and to St Julian made plaint -
saying that this was not what he was fain
to know of faith; however, soon the saint
provided him with lodgings once again.
Within a widow lived, upon whose chain
was kept the keys to every gate and door;
her husband perished lately in the war.

She'd had her maid prepare a bath and meal -
most sumptuous – for her expected lover;
but fortune had been turning back her wheel,
and through a serving-man she did discover
that he'd been called away to some place other -
on urgent business. She resolved instead
to take the bath herself, then go to bed.

The bath she entered in was near the door,
behind which Reynold lay beside the wall -
and soon she heard his weeping full and sore.
Concerned, her maid she summoned from the hall,
and said, when she had answered to her call:
'Kindly see who is at the postern-foot,

while I prepare the supper that was put.'.

The maid went – finding Reynold in his shirt -
and barefoot – in the clear air trembling much,
lying there wretched in the straw and dirt.
She asked him who he was – he told her such -
and of his troubles – which her heart did touch.
Her lady, once informed, was likewise piteous,
and of this handsome stranger curious.

The maid – commending her for her compassion -
let Reynold in; 'Quick – take the bath that's there',
she said, seeing his face from coldness ashen;
while he obeyed, they found him clothes to wear.
Reviving in the warmth, he said a prayer -
thanking St Julian and God for this,
as all around him seemed a scene of bliss.

Within the dining hall was lit a fire,
where sat the lady; soon her maid there came -
and of this stranger's state she did enquire.
'Madam – he's clad himself; he's of good name,
and handsome, with a well-proportioned frame.'.
The lady, hearing this, wished him to meet,
and said: 'Go dear – invite him here to eat.'.

Accordingly, Reynold entered the hall, and saw
the lady, thanking her for kindness done;

she asked how he had come beside the door -
a spirited narration he begun -
how he was robbed beneath the setting sun.
She'd seen his serving-man that day - so true
she thought it, telling Reynold what she knew.

Afterwards, Reynold sat with her to sup.
Her lover gone that night, many a time
she glanced at him while drinking from her cup -
as he was comely, pleasant - in his prime;
her passions roused, she thought them not a crime.
She found her maid in order to confer
if she should use what fortune sent to her.

The maid, who clearly saw her lady's drift,
encouraged her to go, as she could best,
and take advantage of this earthly gift.
Returning to the fireside, where sat her guest,
she gazed on him, filled with romantic zest,
and said: 'Why look you lost and melancholy?
Your stolen things can be requited wholly.

Come now – be comfortable and of good cheer;
take ease, and treat this house as your own place.
I'll tell your something more – to see you here -
a hundred times I've wished you to embrace,
but feared that you would find this a disgrace.
Had I not thought that you might be displeased,

the opportunity I would have seized.'

Reynold advanced on her with open arms,
saying: 'Madam, considering I owe
so much to you, not to enjoy your charms
a great unmanliness in me would show.
Your persuasion is not needed though;
to look upon your face I am content -
there I can see the winning argument.'

No more was said. The lady, full of longing,
straight threw herself at him; many a caress
and kiss each gave - with inner passions thronging -
while now his troubles he could only bless
that brought such moments of expansiveness.
When daylight trickled round the room he rose,
and went to find his servant with his clothes.

The sun was bright, the city gates unlocked,
and searching round his serving-man he found;
he praised St Julian, whom they had mocked,
when next a miracle would him astound.
Those highwaymen appeared, in shackles bound,
arrested by the watchmen for some deed
that same night done – all ended well indeed.

The men confessed – returned his items too;
climbing his horse, he soon forgot his plight,

and homewards rode. To her he bid adieu;
the memories would fill him with delight.
And now so ends my tale of this good knight,
my homely tale of unexpected things -
of how misfortune sometimes fortune brings.

THE CHATELAINE OF CASTLE WILLIAM

'If a bird builds a nest
To lay its eggs in it
Then, it never flies away again
But stays in it
On the eggs in its nest
Even while strangled.'

- the chatelaine's vow.

The moment that I saw – that sombre day -
those stern, forbidding walls that lay ahead,
those lifeless towers that frowned in skies of grey,
those bare and arrow steps that to it led,
those brooding mountains that around it spread -
a mood of inexpressible gloominess -
a palpable, unsettling sense of dread
seemed to seize me - my every thought depress -
my very being - to its core - possess.

The grim, majestic silence of the castle
hung over darksome woods of pine and oak.
One felt the bygone days of alter, vassal
and valour - which the village streets evoke.

THREE TALES

Halting - my horseman - not a word he'd spoke -
had left me near the entrance to its hill.
The featureless facade - where nothing broke
its grave austerity, had made it feel
a thing of fantasy – thing not quite real.

I sojourned then through Europe - in the wake
of revolution lately seen in France,
whose tumult made the ancient order shake
throughout the continent. I took the chance -
while near - to see this relic of romance -
of ages filled with ballads, tales and lore.
Drawn strangely to its bleakness at first glance,
I felt compelled to climb the steps – explore
this vacant pile – to peer beyond the door.

Forcing its blank and sturdy oak, I found
a hall - then inner courtyard. It felt good
to see this tranquil scene that stretched around.
By steep and narrow steps – as best I could -
I trod the winding walkways' creaking wood.
A library with dusty books was crammed;
in eerie stillness suits of armour stood.
The cellars seemed like dungeons of the damned,
another door mysteriously jammed.

Proceeding, labyrinthine passageways
I followed - ducking through doorways as I went.

And while through arrowslits came setting rays,
my curiosity was not content.
Within a chamber - given ornament
by rugs and tapestries - I found a book
that chronicled the castle's turbulent
and frightful history – this tome I took
with candles to the library to look.

It told of bitter, ancient rivalry -
and ghastly acts of vengeance that befell
this troubled house, that plagued its family -
deeds that the keeper of the gates of hell
would loath to look upon. The author well
those stories there relates – of which to hear
he'd sought the castle's chatelaine to tell -
approaching her when death was growing near -
to tell him what she'd seen – which I read here:

'Employed in buildings large and venerable,
a trusted resident - the chatelaine -
attends the kitchen, stable, keep and hall,
and wears her keys around a silver chain.
This household's longest-serving shall remain
unnamed. The feuding family she served -
their savage acts of cruelty – barely sane -
which this her testimony has preserved -
left her profoundly shaken and unnerved.

Within these walls the winds of enmity
would never cease. Two brothers for it fought -
whose sire himself it gained through treachery -
from one whose wife he stole. Wrathful he brought
a curse on his descendants – each who sought
the castle for themselves by evil deeds -
by horrors never known till then - which wrought
their marks upon the stone – which sowed the seeds
for gardens overgrown with snarling weeds.

These brothers - thirsting for each other's blood,
doomed generations since to lustful lives -
their names forever written in the mud -
to murder, incest, lies; to seething hives
of merciless stepmothers, vengeful wives
and jealous husbands - and to plots to win
this stronghold with concealed yet ready knives -
false reconciliations – with any sin
devised as thunder rolled with fearsome din.

One of the brothers took the house by force -
stealing the other's wife – casting him out
in woods to wonder. Pursuing a course
of retribution – caring not to flout
any morality - he set about
to kidnap, kill and cook his children – wait
until he came invited – ease his doubt
if any were – then serve them on a plate,

hiding in food their pieces – which he ate.

The new custodian's oath of duty sworn,
this chatelaine had started here to work.
One day outside, a servant came to warn
her of a door from which all seemed to shirk -
one underground – forgotten in the murk.
Found in a dingy wing, he only knew
that something seemed inside this room to lurk
so disconcerting them - that round it grew
much muttered rumour – not perhaps untrue.

She said: 'Though there was not the faintest trace
of warmth within his few and guarded words -
his stiff and formal air – his rigid face -
he not unfriendly seemed. Suddenly birds
gathered above our heads - and bleating herds
summoned him. Anxious, I was left alone.
At supper, by a fireplace hung with swords,
one evening - I heard a distant moan -
like someone calling in an anguished tone.

Venturing down below to where it came -
or seemed to – coming to a basement room
I'd noticed not before, I heard the same -
a moan which startled me there in the gloom,
moan that could wake the dead within their tomb.
It shook me to the depths - as so appalling

was its sound - then came a tremendous boom -
made by a footstep; noises like fingers scrawling
came next – and haunting cries of children calling.

Disorientated as I fled that scene -
lost in a subterranean dead end,
a single shaft of moonlight I could glean -
and found steps near – which starting to ascend
I saw my way out - and my servant friend.
Then suddenly there came into my mind
that oath – whose sense I did not comprehend
when made. The call of duty I could find
there now – of which it seemed me to remind.

'If a bird builds a nest
To lay its eggs in it
Then, it never flies away again
But stays in it
On the eggs in its nest
Even while strangled.'

Gathering up myself – back then I went,
finding its rusty key. With all my might
the stiff and stubborn handle soon I bent -
and saw there – in the dimness – saw a sight -
a spectral figure that amazed me quite.
Extremely frail he looked – chained on the bed -
hardly more than a skeleton; bone white

his flesh and hair – as if he seldom fed.
I asked him who he was – slowly he said:

'Though for me to speak I've hardly breath -
I'll speak; my name is Skelton, and this place
was mine once. Punishment more harsh than death -
your family's sire that stole it – to disgrace
me all the more – to gloat upon my face -
locked me in here alone. Mine was the curse -
mine the revenge – with which I could debase
his family – to drive to acts perverse -
unnatural – but grudges are as worse.'

I told what happened since their sire had died,
recounting all his children's acts of lust -
which to hear he bowed his head and sighed.
'This much appals me. Yet my chains of rust -
and rage - cause me my pain. To fade to dust
is now my sole escape and wish. To lift -
perhaps - this curse may bring it, and I must -
I made it, only I can heal the rift
and end this torment; so I'll do it swift.'

Since then I'm still the chatelaine of here,
troubled by little but the daily chores,
and things more commonplace that others fear.
Though sometimes I've a presence felt indoors -

sworn   something's   moved   –   imagined   creaking
floors -
my duty calls. The garden, room and lamb -
the dinner and the cellar me implores;
as after all I was – and always am -
the chatelaine of Castle William."

CLORIS AND THE POTION OF LIFE

I have a tale as strange as fantasy -
of deadly passions and possessive rage,
of gains in knowledge thrown in jeopardy -
set in Messina – in the dawning age
of voyages of bold discovery -
of muskets, cannons, and the printed page -
a small and charming city, yet a place
where wild events imperiled once our race.

Alexis was a keen, inquiring sort,
a bachelor that studied medicine -
and he it was, whom creatures – green and short -
were spying on, in hopes by theft to win
a potion that he worked on, which could thwart -
if drank - disease and death. Full was his bin
with failed, discarded formulas – and pale
his skin, from labours yet of no avail.

Another thing had turned his face this hue -
distracting him, depriving him of rest,
of appetite, of any joy he knew
until that day – that day his interest
was caught by her – by Cloris. Though it true

they'd not exchanged a word – it would arrest
his mind to recollect her - make it fraught
with vain hopes – burden every waking thought.

Burden it was to love with little hope,
to struggle with a passion true and pure -
of such a fierceness he could barely cope.
Seen at a service – modest and demure
in bearing, fair in feature – to elope
with her he'd dreamt of nightly - but a cure
he needed now – as soon his dreams were buried -
upon discovering that she was married.

Damon - distinguished in the cavalry,
was this her husband that he envied much.
At other Masses - since that day - he'd see
them stand together – yet her face was such
you would not think her happy. Carelessly
she seemed to glance at him - which brought a touch
of hope - but snatched soon was its gasping breath,
by tidings of her sudden puzzling death.

Plunged into bitter, inconsolable grief -
he shut himself indoors, and would not eat
nor sleep. Mortality – the callous thief
had torn all joy from him. Almost complete
was his formula now, with his belief -
revitalised - that death he soon could cheat -

death he could cheat. The very thought rekindled
his hope for her – whom nature from him swindled.

Galvanized he toiled all day and night,
unresting in his hurried quest to find
the secret to elixir – said to fight
all pains and maladies of humankind.
Patient those gnomes were watching - out of sight -
their eagerness unshakable and blind.
Finally – nearing midnight - he held up
the finished formula inside a cup.

Cloris was buried in her family tomb,
for hours she'd lain inside it undisturbed.
Found at the city's outskirts – it had room
for many occupants. Although perturbed
to think that he a body would exhume,
his apprehensiveness he quickly curbed,
and in the small hours of the next day
he came and through the graveyard made his way.

Her coffin found, slowly he opened it.
To see her - motionless there - made him pause,
made him - overwhelmed with feelings - sit.
Untouched by time, lovely in death she was -
as though she slept. Only his lantern lit
the solemn scene around. Removing the gauze
from off the vial he'd brought, he took the potion

and held it to her lips – but then saw motion.

He saw her move – before a drop she drank -
open her eyes - as death she seemingly shook -
and slowly rise. Startled - he quickly shrank.
Had sleep for death in error been mistook?
What spinner of our fates had he to thank
to see her breathe again? Again to look
on her – and feel his passion burn inside -
which rumour only recently denied.

Looking around the tomb she saw him there -
and her surprise increased when recognition
took hold. Frozen with fear the fated pair
exchanged some glances. Was he an apparition?
she thought, as round her shoulders fell her hair.
He saw no signs of slight decomposition
around her youthful, full and glowing features -
as all the while looked on those impish creatures.

They'd followed him unnoticed to her grave,
scheming to seize the mixture when they could.
These dwellers of the earth would such things crave
to benefit themselves – and little understood
what paths to sure destruction they might pave
for those that dare to dabble. Hushed they stood -
after they'd scurried through their native earth,
where guarding goldmines is their task from birth.

Unknown to him in secret she had felt
a passion for him equal to his own.
The serpent love within her daily dwelt,
and many times she gave a stifled groan
to see him, while her sighing heart would melt.
Gladdened to find herself with him alone -
she asked him who he was, and why he came;
he then began to speak – though half in shame:

'Alexis is my name. Madam, excuse
any presumption on my part - I meant
not to alarm you. I had heard sad news
of your untimely passing. Not content
to think your lovely features I might lose
forever – with this drink I came - intent
in testing it on you. I find you though -
alive - your hue unchanged; how is this so?'

'You may not know my husband' – then she said,
'My marriage was arranged to Damon. Him
my parents chose - unhappy I was wed.
A victim to his every mood and whim
I sought escape from misery – which led
to drinking herbs that freeze up every limb,
bringing a lifeless sleep. So dead I seemed.
Entombed - to live in happiness I dreamed.'

They held each other, giving much expression
to surging feelings long suppressed within.
Alexis soon forgot his deep depression
to think that his desire he seemed to win.
He lay the potion down. To take possession -
a gnome trod near – as soundless as a pin.
Suddenly footsteps came around the door -
and looking up – entwined – they Damon saw.

'What scene is this on which I make intrusion?
I come to pay my last respects, and yet -
find that the dead is living? An illusion
perhaps? And who is this? My friend - we've met
before, I think.', he said with grave expression.
'My wife you wish? Well - this you will regret.'
He drew his sword and struck him in the chest;
down fell Alexis, while his wound he pressed.

As Damon left them, Cloris held her lover -
bleeding and gasping, he could barely speak.
His mortal injury she tried to cover -
he pointed to the vial while growing weak.
She understood his sense - but going over
to bring this only cure – she gave a shriek.
Belonging to a gnome – a tiny hand
appeared, and snatched the mixture as it planned.

Pursuing hastily the gnome outside,

she wandered round the tranquil cemetery.
Hearing the sound of giggles hushed and snide -
she searched its paths and saw a sturdy tree,
and there behind its trunk the creature spied -
where many more had gathered round to see
this healing drink. Upon a mound he held
the mixture high, and wild with rapture yelled:

'This medicine', he said, 'will give us life
eternal – with which we can build our empire -
expand our goldmines – ease our daily strife.
Its properties will mean we'll never tire,
never be injured by the axe or knife,
or accident of earthquake, flood or fire.'
Cloris – in overhearing this - with dread
was greatly filled, and interrupting said:

'I'm begging you – give me this liquid back;
my friend within is injured – only this
can save him from that unprovoked attack.'
He stood beside the hole to an abyss -
where lay their tunnels - of the blackest black -
and took a sip – with eyes that told of bliss.
Excited, all the gnomes watched on, as he
laughed with malevolent, unruly glee.

'Now I'm a god of gods, a king of kings',
he cried, while inching near the burrow's edge.

'Invincible, fearing naught, now I have wings -
I'm like a bird upon a window ledge.'
Not watching where he danced, looking at things
not there – he raised the vial as if to pledge
some oath to someone – as if under spell -
then lost his footing – dropped the glass – and fell.

Hearing his fading echo, Cloris saw
the vessel and retrieved it from the ground.
Some mixture it contained still. This she bore
back to the mausoleum, where she found
Alexis barely breathing. Trying to pour
some potion in his mouth, a coughing sound
she heard, then saw his still and bloodied lips
moving. He woke – and took some further sips.

Watching his wounds like magic disappear,
Alexis stood and held her. Cloris told
of what had happened then, of which to hear
he took the glass and said: 'It may bring gold
for some - but also dangers - which I fear.
And so - I must destroy this stuff I hold.
Come now, and while we can let's leave here fast.'
So saying went they, hand in hand at last.

9 781068 666636